MW01060518

The Twelve Dancing Princesses

Once upon a time in a faraway kingdom, there lived a king who had twelve beautiful daughters. The king loved his daughters very much, and was very protective of them. And so, he made his daughters all sleep in one room, with a door that locked from the outside.

Curiously, every morning the shoes of the twelve princesses were always well worn—as if they had been danced in all night! But every night, the king saw that no one left or entered their room.

Utterly stumped, the king let it be known across the land that whoever could solve the mystery of the worn shoes could marry the princess of his choosing!

A prince arrived at the castle, and he was taken to the chamber next to the princesses' room, where he could watch and listen. But the prince fell asleep, and when he awoke, he could not explain where the princesses had gone, or how their shoes had become so worn.

After this prince came another, and then a nobleman. They both quickly fell asleep, and the princesses' shoes were even more worn than ever the next day! The king became frustrated, and banished them all.

Meanwhile, a poor soldier heard about the mystery of the worn shoes, and the reward of marrying a princess! The soldier was brave and cunning, and liked to solve puzzles. And so he set off toward the castle, determined to solve the mystery himself. While walking through the woods, the soldier suddenly heard a cry for help.

He ran toward the sound, and saw an old woman crying out for help in a river. The current was very quick, and she would soon be swept away! The soldier grabbed a branch, and held it out to the woman.

"Grab hold!" he called, and with his quick thinking and strength, she was saved.

Together, they built a fire, and the soldier gave the old woman his cloak to warm up. They began to talk, and the soldier confessed that he was going to the castle to solve the puzzle of the twelve princesses and their worn-out shoes.

"If you are going to uncover their secret, you will need some help," said the old woman.

The old woman was really a sorceress! She pulled the soldier's cloak over her head, and whispered some mysterious words. It was now a magical cloak that turned the wearer invisible!

"How can I ever thank you?" asked the soldier, admiring the cloak.

"Your kindness and bravery saved my life. I am repaying the favor," replied the sorceress. "But be warned, do not drink anything the princesses offer you, for it will surely put you to sleep!"

The next morning, the soldier and the sorceress parted ways. They wished each other well, and the soldier set off toward the castle. He ran through the forest as fast as he could, so that he would be sure to arrive before the princesses went to bed.

The soldier received a royal welcome at the castle. Just like the princes and nobleman before him, the soldier was told to spend the night in the room next to the bedchamber of the twelve mysterious princesses.

As the soldier looked around, the eldest of the twelve princesses entered the room.

"Welcome," said the princess, "please, have a glass of wine."

The soldier remembered the sorceress's warning, and poured the wine into a plant as the princess left. He then lay down, and began snoring loudly.

When the princesses heard the snoring, they all jumped out of bed and began to change into their prettiest gowns and jewels. But the youngest princess was unsure, and told her sister that she was worried.

"Don't worry, little sister," said the eldest princess, "my sleeping potion has put many men to sleep!"

Seeing that her sister was still worried, the two princesses went to the room next door. The soldier appeared to be fast asleep, with the empty wineglass nearby.

It's too bad he'll be banished in the morning, thought the eldest princess, *he looks quite charming!*

Reassured, the two princesses returned to their room. The soldier silently put on the magic cloak and tiptoed behind them.

Inside the princesses' bedchamber, the carpet in the center of the room had been rolled up. The eldest princess stood above it and clapped her hands three times.

Clap, clap, clap!

Then she tapped her foot three times.

Tap, tap, tap!

On the third tap of her foot, a door opened, revealing a hidden staircase

16

The eldest princess went down the staircase first, followed by her eleven sisters. The soldier rushed behind them and accidentally stepped on the youngest princess's dress.

"There's someone here! Someone just stepped on my dress," cried the youngest princess.

"Your dress must have gotten snagged on a nail, there's no one there," replied the eldest.

At the bottom of the stairs, the princesses and the soldier stepped out into a grove of sparkling trees with beautiful silver leaves. The soldier knew he would need proof, and snapped off a branch.

"Did you hear that?" called the youngest princess.

"Don't worry, little sister," comforted the eldest, "one of us must have stepped on a twig."

The soldier followed the skipping and twirling princesses, and soon they were in a new grove of trees with gleaming gold leaves. Over the hill, the leaves of other trees shone like sparkling diamonds.

The soldier took a branch from each kind of tree. When the youngest princess heard the snapping of branches, her elder sister reassured her. The eldest princess was sure that her younger sister was scared and imagining things.

The twelve princesses arrived at a lake, where twelve boats with twelve princes were waiting for them! The soldier carefully stepped into the last boat, and joined the youngest princess and prince.

"I must be tired tonight," said the young prince. "We're going slower than the others, and the boat seems heavier than usual."

The boats arrived at the shore of a great castle. The soldier followed the princesses into a beautiful ballroom.

The princesses began to dance. They waltzed and leaped, and swayed and twirled. With all their dancing, their shoes began to wear out. The soldier had solved the mystery of the shoes!

When they grew tired from dancing, they drank from shining gold cups. The soldier took one of the golden cups, as more proof of where they had been.

As dawn approached, the princesses left the way they came, and the soldier followed them back. He slipped into the other room and pretended to be asleep. Before long, he heard the sound of voices.

"You see," said the eldest princess to the youngest, "he is still sound asleep, and our secret is safe."

Later that morning, the soldier was called before the king.

"Do you know why my daughters' shoes are worn to pieces every morning?" asked the king.

The soldier told the story of the trap door, the magical forest, the golden cups, and the dancing in the ballroom. He offered the gleaming twigs and the golden cup as proof.

The princesses were very surprised, but they couldn't deny the truth.

The king was so relieved to have solved the mystery that he wasn't mad at his daughters for sneaking away! The king then asked the soldier which princess he would like to marry.

"Your Majesty, the princesses are all beautiful, but the eldest is also clever, adventurous, and kind!" said the soldier.

The eldest princess was delighted, and they were soon married. At their wedding, they had a grand ball all night, where they danced until their shoes wore out.